ALL THIS LOVE

JASIYAH SHERRIEFF BEY

Studio of Books LLC
5900 Balcones Drive Suite 100
Austin, Texas 78731
www.studioofbooks.org
Hotline: (254) 800-1183

Ordering Information:
Special discounts are available on quantity purchases by corporations, associations, and others. For details, contact the publisher at the address above.

Printed in the United States of America.

ISBN-13: Softcover   978-1-964864-96-9
          eBook   978-1-964864-97-6

Library of Congress Control Number: 2024926517

CONTENTS

Dedication

This book is dedicated to the woman who gave me life and carried me for 9 months. My mother, Johnnie Mae McKinney. You were the source of strength I rely on the most. You are constantly in my thoughts. Every day, I reflect on your life in a magnificent manner. Mother, your influence on my life has been pivotal, and I appreciate your overwhelming faith in me. My objective is to honor you by living an upright life to the fullest extent of my abilities. You have always found joy in the many works I have contributed to throughout my life. Although we had inspirational conversations about this book. You didn't live long enough to see it completed. Mama, you are familiar with my spirit my capabilities of finishing any task placed before me. Even though I miss you very much, I recognize that there are laws in place to distinguish between life and death. I am grateful to Allah for what you have given me. As long as I am alive, you will remain in my thoughts. Take pleasure in your rest because you have worked hard all your life and deserve it.

Johnnie Mae McKinney
(Roberson)
July 31,1938 - July 3, 2024

My Mother

Acknowledgment

It is important for me to acknowledge all the individuals who have had a positive influence on me throughout my life. Despite being anonymous, your influence on my life is still evident today. Your actions or words are present in my mind. Despite the distance between us in this day and time. My thoughts are always with you. I am grateful to all the people who have had a negative impact on my life over the years. My drive to succeed and develope have been influenced by your actions and words. You may have encouraged me to embark on a journey that I never would have dreamed. I want to convey that same level of respect to you. Receiving positive energy is crucial for my strength and faith in my abilities. Negative energy is created to divert my attention and cause me to lose focus. I have gained confidence in my abilities. The purpose of the negative energy is to impede my ability to focus and believe in myself. By conquering that negative energy, my strength grows even stronger. You deserve praise for doing the job you were supposed to do.

Introduction

All of this love is a symphony of life experiences that I have seen and experienced. Broken homes and loneliness can be attributed to a corrupt and lazy conception of love. Couples are remaining together, unhappy and dissatisfied with each other, and raising children in an environment of corrupt ideology of love. It's important to remember that our lives have an impact on what we learn, and that children are being taught a flawed concept of love. What are the means by which they can manifest within? What is the true meaning of love and being loved? A girl who is without a father figure may look for one in a man. In the event that this woman is being abused by a man and she allows the abuse, she allows the corrupt idea of love to evolve in her life. A boy who doesn't have a father figure may struggle with the idea of showing affection. It's conceivable that he witnessed his mother working tirelessly to provide for the whole family without any assistance. At home, the mother was the most powerful and dominant force. What is the potential outcome of this? What are the consequences of a young boy growing up with this example in his life? In life, love is something we all long for and seek. The perfect love story is something everyone aspires to experience. Living with an extraordinary way of life and love necessitates a lot of discipline, practice, work, and understanding.

All This Love

Love! A woman expresses her love for her man, and he replies that he loves you too or that he loves you even more! The husband expresses his love for his wife, and in return, she expresses her love for him beyond that of any other woman. Freely and at the most economical cost, this term of great affection is used. At times, we speak to make others feel good or to make our own egos feel good. During my teenage years, the password to sleep with a girl was 'I love you'. Young teenage boys were walking around saying, "I love you" to some teenage girl with the intention of sleeping with her. In the event that she accepts, he would ultimately say, 'Baby, I love you.' Girl, it's impossible for you to grasp just how much I love you. This situation escalated significantly. As she observes him in ecstasy, she expresses her love for him with a smile on her face. She ponders, I got this one. Adolescents are already being exposed to a flawed conception of love. Do we truly comprehend the words that we teach our children when they are babies? They end up using these words in a cheap manner and do not do anything to support what they truly mean. I have a strong love for you, and I desire the best for everyone except myself. Consequently, all those around you who accept your concept of love take you for granted. You don't need to do anything for them if your love for them is enough.

If you decide against doing it for them in one day. Their feelings of resentment and hostility toward you are manifested. Your love is only possible if you meet certain conditions. If you refuse to do what I ask, my love may turn into an intense dislike until you comply with my demands. Can I express all this love for everyone, and disregard love for my self? Is it possible to love others more than you love yourself? Be generous and extravagant in your affection for others, but be stingy and uncaring in your affection for yourself. Self-esteem can be at the root of why we don't express self-love towards ourselves. Drifting like dust into the wind. I had no direction whatsoever. My lack of discipline was apparent. My lower nature or lower desire was the driving force behind my actions. Wherever the wind blows, there are floating particles of matter and falling dust. For a considerable amount of time, this was me. I was doing nothing for myself. I'm just trying to have sex, confusing it with love. I had the impression that it was love when it took place. When I was younger, I recall asking my cousin Robin "Porky" Roberson? How can you determine if you're in love? She told me that you just know. I have spent a significant amount of time writing songs about love and sex. I'm attempting to comprehend. The truth is, I was searching for something beyond myself. I was trying to find love in all the wrong places. I had no idea that the thing I wanted most was lying dormant within me. What was the reason for my eagerness to learn about love? Perhaps the sting of black inferiority was born after discovering slavery and witnessing the cruel and dehumanizing treatment of slaves. This gave me an internal experience of the pain that my ancestors had to endure. I was capable of feeling what they were feeling and felt that I was not good enough. I experienced feelings of being unattractive and incompetent. Failure to complete my homework resulted in me failing school. I had no expectation of graduating from school. I was under the impression that I couldn't do anything good in my life or survive in this world. I recall being apprehensive about going to school because I would often be made fun of. Today, it is referred to as bullying. I did not have any desire to attend school at all. I would rather spend my time at home watching 'The Brady Bunch' on TV. As I watched, I became very hungry. During my childhood, the refrigerator in my house had very little food.

My thoughts would be, 'I'm hungry.' Food is always in the fridge for them. A house that is nice, a family, and a maid with a fridge full of food. I was perplexed as to why I was born into this life under these circumstances. In that moment, all I wanted was some delicious food. Even though my older sister was in charge of making our family's meals. In those days, watching food on television was more of a delight. Despite everything, I still miss the taste of her fried chicken rice and gravy. Whenever we didn't have gravy, we were content with butter and salt. We were not experiencing illness or death due to hunger. I made the decision to go to school as I knew I would have lunch at school. This was the beginning of a lack of love for me. My mother did her best to make my living conditions as comfortable as possible. It is now clear to me that she made the most of what she had at the time. My perception at that moment was not allowing me to accept my mother's best efforts. It is my assumption that the condition of life was caused by the slavery of black people. I was not able to love myself enough to believe I was valuable. I believed that I was a person who was ugly and unworthy. This was just the beginning of a journey that was filled with loveless moments in my life. From where did that idea originate? My parents never taught me how to feel that way. Maybe my siblings never caused me to feel that way. Where did the notion of being worthless, devalued, and ugly originate? It is a result of a thousand words that I couldn't write or pronounce. At school, it is taught that an image can contain thousands of words. Seeing these images of slavery always brings a thousand words to my soul in a highly subliminal way. The pictures showed slaves who had little food to eat. Their clothing was too big, and most had not had their hair washed or groomed. What's the sublimation statement for me to interpret this image. I did not feel a sense of love for it. The perpetrators of this act had a clear understanding of their actions when they commercialized this symbol of slavery worldwide. The idea of placing black people in danger before they entered the world was masterfully conceived and conveyed. This was global bullying. The United States of America is responsible for the origin of this way of life.

The perpetrators of this cruel way of life lack genuine love for themselves. The act of killing me and my people can be done easily. According to some, there is a slight distinction between love and hate. It's like a string with love and hatred on either side, ready to go to war. People celebrate the sweetness of the voice that whispers love, but love is not a soft word. The things you see on TV or social media can make us think differently. Love is defined as a powerful feeling of deep affection. Love demands a certain level of commitment, discipline, engagement, and practice. The act of love involves a series of actions that reinforce character, relationships, marriages, and the way people communicate with one another. Love is a genuine expression of truth, and it's not possible to whisper truth to somebody you love. Love's truth emerges strong and fierce, like the sound of a brass trumpet when it's played in front of you. The sound of that triggers the nervous system, requiring your full attention. The truth of love is the same when spoken in strong and unadulterated words, without any sweetness.

We are drawn to a foolish way of loving each other. As we move towards this corrupted concept of love. Our actions towards revealing the truth are characterized by weakness and cowardice. This act of weakness and cowardice lacks love. We have all been actors and actresses in love. We are fond of the thought of what we perceive as love in our minds. That thought has nothing to do with love. It's nothing more than a fantasy. I'm still waiting for a birthday card from you. You never provided me with what I needed to satisfy my selfish approach to the concept of love. You're unwilling to love me because money is important to me and you don't have any. It's true, you make me feel special. Your manners are very polite. You show gentleness and respect towards my feelings, ideas, and opinions. It's not good enough. "I want a ruff neck." A young woman who was beautiful told me that one day. I am a friend. I found her to be incredibly beautiful and she remains so to this day. We conversed extensively. I had an enjoyable time with her. Her mother recognized my affection for her daughter. She was starting to realize that I had a desire to be her man. I expressed this as if I were an adult, even though I was still in my teenage years. A boy who thinks like a man, whatever that signifies.

I had a strong affection for her. In spite of this, she was involved in an abusive relationship. My presence was meant to offer a listening ear and be a genuine friend. I kept in mind that if that guy makes a mistake, I would be there to handle the aftermath. One day, she informed me that she was ready for me. It was a happy day for me. For the first time, we exchanged a kiss. I was filled with excitement inside because this was the day I had been anticipating for years. We kissed, and right in the midst of that passionate kiss.

She stopped me and declared that she was unable to do this. My face bore an idiotic expression. I said, Can you explain? Just calm down and let's do it again. I was ready to begin singing with the voice of Mavis Staples, "Shamone". The word "Shamone," popularized by Michael Jackson in songs like "Bad," is a tribute to Mavis Staples' vocal riff in "I'll Take You There".

I was certain that I wasn't going crazy. I was captivated by the passion in that kiss. We are only a short distance away from elevating this to the next level. It was a hot summer day. She expressed her inability to proceed with this. But the respect I have for her allows me to remain calm. As a result, I stopped basing myself on her, and I had to ask. Was the kiss unpleasant? I expressed my desire to try it again. I wasn't planning on giving up just yet. She communicated these words to me. You are incredibly sweet and kind. But I need a ruffneck. At that moment, I expressed my gratitude to MC Lyte. My mind was prepared for love by listening to R&B soul and love songs. Hip hop prepared her mind for what she wanted out of a man. We both had this idea of a fantasy love in our minds.

In the book of 1 Corinthians in the King James Version of the Holy Bible it reads; Love is patient and sweet, not jealous, not bragging, not proud, Rude or selfish, not easily angry, and it keeps no trace of wrongdoing. Love does not gloat about others' sins but takes pleasure in the truth. Love always supports, always trusts, always hopes, always endures. Love does not end; When you examine the verse mentioned above about love. Answers are being provided with words that create ideas and images of what real love can be if exercised.

I love him

Although you're confused, you still say you love this guy. Despite your suffering, you persist in declaring your love for him. This man speaks to you in a harsh manner. He uses derogatory names to refer to you whenever he's not getting what he wants. He is like a boy who is spoiled and has difficulty getting what he wants from his mother. He comes after you with fury and a distasteful tone. Within hours, he apologized for his behavior. You claim to have feelings for him and say, 'I love him.' You really need to learn to love yourself above anyone else. You engage in a vicious love cycle. What is the true criterion for love? Do we rely on our feelings, emotions, good sex, and imagination for love? I am overwhelmed by this unpleasant situation. Despite being in a cloud of negativity, we are foolishly unaware of what we think is love. What is the genuine standard of love? Does it revolve around feelings, emotions, good sex, or the love ideas in your imagination? I am confused by this unfortunate situation. We are immersed in negativity, but we are unaware of what we believe love is. I have the choice to stay or leave. There are indications of progress. Although he treats you coldly, you have a strong attachment to him. For some reason or another, you believe that you can handle the abuse. Your emotions are played like a violin, and you're deceived by the highly emotional sensation you believe is love. These words are sung by Regina Belle in her song 'This Is Love'. This is love. Ooh, I think I'm falling for you. These emotions, feelings, and excitement are what I feel. The feeling of love must be present.

Then she goes on to sing 'Ooh,' an exclamation used to convey a range of emotions, including surprise, pleasure, or pain. It could also indicate that I am doing something wrong or that I should not be doing it in the first place. Then she says, 'I think I'm falling for you.' I'm falling in love with you, even though it's not something I know for sure. Emotional confusion is present in this moment. Her only concern is falling in love with someone other than herself. Falling is an adjective that means going from a higher level to a lower level generally quickly and uncontrollably. Love is defined by these negative attributes that we associate with it. Next, we develop a delusional notion of what we consider love to be. Debra Laws sings these words in her song 'Very Special.' "Love is life, and life is living." Life is the existence of an individual human being or animal. We need to love our lives, love ourselves, be truthful to ourselves, and live our lives in truth.

Beyond Love

Debarge, a family vocal group, sings, "All this love is waiting for you." The concept of love has been shaped by music, movies, and television. How love is perceived and conveyed and what our thoughts are about it. Being loved is a fundamental human need. Who doesn't want to be loved by someone? Who doesn't want to hear the words 'I love you'? We all desire to feel those emotions at some point in our lives. This love scene is defined through the lens of movies and soap operas. The telenovelas that are truly dramatic. Telenovelas are known for their continuous melodramatic storyline and constant cast. You can easily become addicted to this drama. Although I watched it, I couldn't speak or understand Spanish at the time. No digo que ahora se hablar español con fluidez. Sólo entiendo una o dos palabras. I'm not implying that I speak Spanish fluently right now. I only understand one or two words. Learning a different language is made easy by these apps nowadays. At the age of 13, I began writing songs about love. My inner desires and fetishistic fantasies about love and romance. This concept of love has been incorporated into my mind. When this thought was not aligned with the actions of the young woman. I began to search for the corrupted notion of love in another young woman. That consistent pattern of love failing was all I knew. So, with this failed mental imprint of love, came failed relationships, one after the other.

Her

In the past, I would obsess over love in my mind. I made an effort to convey it as best as I could. And that's when I first met her. She was incredibly beautiful. A young woman who is intelligent and attractive. However, she was very reserved and sophisticated, and I didn't want to do anything but look at her smile. Seeing how young we were, she looked like an adult woman in a teenage body. Her older sisters were similarly shaped with curves in the appropriate places, like her. She was just a younger version of them. In my mind like Florida Evans, I yelled, "Dam, dam, dam!" They set the rules before allowing me to date their baby sister. Her family was a source of love for me. I heard the words of my cousin Robin "Porky" Roberson whisper in my mind, 'You know, when you fall in love." Towards the end of summer 1985, I was employed at Burger King. I comprehend your thoughts, how can a 15-year-old who was about to turn 16 work at Burger King? I had the ability to age on my birth certificate by using the Jedi mind trick. I had no social security number whatsoever. Now you comprehend that magic trick. Keep in mind that I didn't fall from heaven. I acquired the skill of climbing through the abyss of America. During that same year my friends and I started a dance group that ultimately turned into a singing group. A friend of mine introduced me to her. I was told that she's a family girl, so don't you attempt to sleep with her. Now I said, Why would you think something like that. He said, 'Pee McNasty, I know you; I'm your boy.' We gave each other some dap, laughed, and said, 'True dat!'. It's necessary to acknowledge that my friends and I were over-sexualized teens. It was Wometco Home Theater (WHT). Yes, this is the initial pay TV service in the New York area. We stayed awake past midnight to watch what was referred to as a nightcap. The next day, we gathered around to discuss what we saw in the previous episode.

Taking notes to describe the sex pleasures we have to experience with the girls in our neighborhood. You observe the game's design. Our sexual promiscuity was highly intensified. Even though we were adolescents, we were a good group of young black men. In spite of the political views regarding the youth of Black Americans. Politicians had the audacity to label black youth as 'predictors', making us an easy target for death. A predator is a noun, predators is a plural noun which is an animal that naturally preys on others. A person who ruthlessly exploits others. I am aware that the brothers and sisters in the area did not meet the criteria of predators. So why would white politicians go to such lengths to label black youth in that manner? It seems like they became a part of the 'All This Love' series. For their diabolical schemes of being the destructive creature of anyone who produces love, justice, or equality of any kind. Let's get back on topic. We didn't understand these sex-crazed fantasies and misinterpreted them as love? In spite of all my flaws, it was a natural thing for me to treat her in the best possible way. I had no idea what the most suitable course of action was. It was my natural instinct to know that it was the right thing to do.

A Beautiful Moment in Time

One day, she informed me that she had met my father. He worked at a store located just a few blocks away from where she lived. She entered the store along with her two older sisters. When my father saw her, he expressed his admiration for her beauty. He said, "You are so purty, my son would love you." Due to my sense of humor, I asked her to come with me to the store where my father works and follow my lead. My plan was to go to the store and have a conversation with my dad. Within two minutes, have her enter after me. As if she just happened to show up at that time. As I conversed with my father, he began to speak with enthusiasm about this beautiful young woman. After a few minutes, she happened to be walking into the store. My father was filled with excitement. Monk, that is her!

There she goes, there she goes, that's her. I paused and glanced over at her. I placed my hand on my father's shoulder and declared, "I'll be back as soon as I can." He was most likely contemplating in his mind.

Respectfully, grab hold of that gorgeous and provocative young lady and hold on to her, son. Because in truth, her presence demands nothing less. I told my dad I'll be right back. I walked over to create the impression that we were having a conversation. That's when I gave her a kiss. My father gazed at me with a surprise expression on his face. He shouted, 'You son of a gun!' Whenever you played a joke on him, he would always say, 'You son of a gun.' We laughed hysterically, and I introduced him to her. I found this moment to be wonderful. It was blissful, and love was in the air. This moment was truly beautiful.

Dreadful Day

Then came the dreadful day. Her parents have purchased a home, and she is moving to a different state. We were both completely devastated. I've had the most amazing six months of my life, and it's about to end as a result. Yeah, I know you are probably saying 6 months. That 6 months laid a foundation for the most beautiful experience of my life and that is about to end. I remember the day so well. The weather was cloudy and humid. She would say goodbye to her family and friends. We used the dollar van to go to her house for the last time. During our time in the van, we were not too talkative. Holding hands in a state of sadness. Then Whitney Houston's 'All At Once' began to play on the radio. At that time, I felt emotionally devastated and hurt. When it was time for us to bid farewell. I found this to be the hardest thing to do at that time in my life. I recall being in a car with her family as we made our way to the airport. The silence was so intense that we didn't speak at all. I was gazing out the window and trying to suppress my tears. Her sister looked over and said, 'Pee, are you okay?' I wiped my tears and said, 'Yes, I am a man, I will be alright.' Nah! I did not say that! I just nodded my head yes, wiping my runny nose and tears.

At the airport I could barely look at her. I was so angry that she was leaving. The moment the plane took off, I went into survival mode. I had to be dropped off by her older sister because she stayed behind while the family went ahead. She asked me if I was okay, and I replied with vigor and anger. I won't divulge to you what transpired next. But let's just say I was out of my mind. When she was gone, I would listen to 'All At Once' every once in a while to relive the emotions and pain I felt that day. It is evident that music plays a role in the presence of love. The absence of love makes it even more important. Music and the longing to fall in love with someone. Has a significant effect on our state of mind and emotions. It reflects on the way we live in our minds. The realm of our imagination is where we live and experience love. Hopeful, eager, and seeking love. It's conceivable to confuse the greatest emotional stimulation with the greatest feelings of love. While we continue down this path of corrupt love. We are facing a great deal of trouble. Whether I stay or leave, I'll find the right reason to stay and the wrong reason to leave in such a confused state. We make the assumption that I am in love when we are not even aware of the kind of love we are actually enslaved by. Someone who is confined or feels confined is considered a prisoner. Imprisoned by a situation or set of circumstances. How many of us experience this type of relationship in our lives? He and she have both been abusive. Our objective is to put an end to this narcissistic relationship with this individual. They act as if they were always right, that they knew better, and that their partner was wrong or incompetent. This often leaves the other person in the relationship angry and trying to defend themselves, or relating this to a negative self-image and feelings about themselves. We shouldn't be living our lives like that. Due to our limited time in life, we tend to prioritize other people's feelings over our own. We are destroyed by love because we lack understanding of it.

Love Yourself

I wrote a song called "Love Yourself" across all streaming channels. When that song manifested, I had been out of the recording loop for more than 10 years. My music producer, one of the most empowering brothers I know, is the one I look to most as a friend and a producer. He always brings out the best in me. This brother has been like this since we met when I was 19 years old. I told him I lost it because I hadn't written a song in over 10 years. Look at his words. "Take your time and allow the words to manifest in your being." During my repeated listening of the track, I heard the words "Love Yourself" manifest.

The lyrics are like:

You are great, you are love, you are beautiful.

The power to change, comes from within.

You been told, many things that wasn't true.

Through it all, held it down, it's time now.

You can do it, love yourself, don't let nobody take that from you.

You can do it, just be, let love live right through you, love yourself

Your a King, your a Queen, you are a God.

The power to change is in your hands.

You been told many things, to keep you down.

Through it all, you keep moving.

You can do it, love yourself, don't let nobody take that from you.

You can do it, just be, let love live right through you, love yourself.

You can do it, you can do it, you can do it

love yourself

(Rap)

Know why I was told that,

I'm a nigger and I always be that,

got my hands and feet nailed to the cross,

I'm the one in the wilderness lost,

take back my righteous mind,

this is my time to shine,

the God is waking up,

black God is waking up.

By the time I've finished recording that song. I was taken aback by the ease with which my inner spirit gave me those words. It was like I was given a present with every word written in the song. I was truly amazed at the way those powerful words manifested in me. The only thing I had to do was play my song 'Love Yourself'. Listening to that song always brings me back to the energy of the moment it was written. Loving yourself, for the most part, is quite difficult when you have been mentally brainwashed into believing and falling into the trap of corrupt love in regard to self-love. It's commonly believed that God is love. Without the knowledge of God, how can a man, woman, boy, or girl comprehend love? What is the real extent of our knowledge and understanding of love? What is the actual extent of our knowledge and wisdom about love? Is it accurate to view love as an emotion? Ms. Tina Turner sang, 'What's love got to do with it?' 'What's love but a second-hand emotion.' Is love truly an emotion that can be secondhand? What is the definition of a secondhand emotion? An emotion that passes quickly or is not useful is often referred to as a secondhand emotion. It's similar to second-hand stories that's derived from something we acquire from others, but that we don't directly feel ourselves.

The magical land of our imagination is where love is experienced, as if it were real. When your husband, wife, boyfriend, or girlfriend fails to live up to the ideals of love in your imagination. There is a significant amount of trouble in the water. Having a fight, yelling, and screaming that you don't love me leads to the other person losing their mind and becoming crazy. It doesn't matter what I did or didn't do to make you feel this way. They become so engrossed in their love imagination that they have predetermined thoughts of physically harming or killing the person they claim to love so much. What internal processes are responsible for allowing a feeling, emotion, or thought to push us to our limits? We want to destroy someone because our emotions are hurt. What triggers our weakness and emotional attachment to secondhand emotions that we mistake for love? Luther Ingram sang, 'If loving you is wrong, I don't want to be right.' What's wrong with this picture right here? Being right isn't important to me if loving you is wrong. Brother is in a situation he should not be in. Despite the fact that this love is already showing signs of corruption, he doesn't care about being right. He persists in loving the wrong way because he wants to avoid being wrong. Does she have a significant other? Loving her is not a good idea and you don't want to be right because it would mean you couldn't be with her anymore. A selfish and corrupt idea of love. Taking a hard look at our acts of love can result in us accepting it from the start. Our priority is love, not respect. The expression of love is present, but there is no respect between them. If this is the scenario that you are experiencing, then you must understand that love is absent. How can you be in love with someone while also disrespecting them? During that moment, discipline comes into play. There are moments when you want to use derogatory language towards him or her. Calling each other outside of their names. The only reason you don't do so is because people are around you, and you must protect your self-image. The only thing you are acquiring are skills to safeguard the falsehood you are upholding. To train yourself to use appropriate words to show respect to yourself and others. This would be fantastic if it were the case.

The Things I Heard This Man Speak

The words that this man spoke to a woman. This man who appears to be certain of himself. Frequently harasses this woman about the same scenario that she gave him all the answers to repeatedly. He acts as if he was the coolest man on the planet earth.

He was in the midst of planning his future with this woman, and they were just beginning their relationship. By making all of these preparations for their life together, he expressed his love for her. The one thing that was somewhat perplexing for me to accept. How was he planning their lives without her present to hear them? Throughout my observation of him, I found myself shaking my head. He fabricated his belief that he was deeply in love. He behaved like a gentleman by being very attentive to her. In his view, he is a well-trained and disciplined person who can use the English vernacular on command. Brother is truly in denial and don't realize it. In life, we have all had the opportunity to get ourselves somewhat dirty. I recognize that I have encountered numerous unfavorable circumstances in my life. I will not pretend to be anything I am not. If that's the case, I'll let you know. Yes, I did this or that and became the black sheep. Jermaine Jackson once said, "Why do we build this castle of sand. When we know very well, baby, it will never stand? I have built numerous castles out of sand. Building love on a sand castle is what we do. When we are certain that it won't stand or hold. The world of love is being fed to our minds through television and movies, which we are beginning to deceive ourselves into. Is this understanding of love rooted in science or emotions? For prolonged periods of time, emotions can cause us to move in the wrong direction. Does this explain the high rate of divorce or separation in every relationship or marriage we see today? What is their perception of love after a divorce, separation, or breakup of the family if they are involved? What is the impact of this drama on their mental capacity when it comes to love? Should they start learning love from a scientific perspective or continue down the path of corrupt love and end up at the same destination? I encountered a woman for the first time in my life, and she mentioned that she had a dream about me before we met. I am still amazed that I was fooled by that nonsense. I got sucked into that toxic idea of love that was driven by sexuality when I saw a big butt and a smile.

How will you bounce back from the pain of love

What steps can you take to bounce back from the pain of love or the pain of corrupt love? We must learn to control our emotions with intelligence. We cannot and should not ride the emotional tidal wave and believe that we will arrive safely on a beautiful sandy beach. How can I protect myself from being hurt by someone? The only option is to love yourself so much that when someone hurts you, you can take it all in stride. I have a good grasp of the motivation behind that person's actions, but not the motive behind their actions towards me. What has happened to them in their life that has made it hard for them to love others and love themselves? The acts of unselfishness they committed are done without any effort. They lack any indication of remorse for their actions. If our love for God and ourselves is genuine.

We will learn to resist the emotional roller coaster of corrupt love. Love can be practiced and treated like a science. Science is the most mathematical subject in school past and present. Science is the subject that is most accurate in both school and life. Despite this, a significant number of students reject it. If we desire to gain knowledge about love from a scientific and mathematical perspective. The analytical analysis of our new scientific and mathematical approach to love would have to take precedence over our emotional perception. Many couples are no longer able to sustain their marriages. For those involved in marriage or relationships who are capable of coping with the difficult times and have put in the effort. You are not the focus of this. We can draw lessons from your experience on how to overcome difficulties in love, marriage, and life. In today's society, the average lifespan of a marriage is between 3 and 6 years. The law has established marriage as a business agreement. It seems to me that marriage is meant to be for love. If there is a divorce, the man must either pay alimony, child support, or give up half. Women are now being hit with the same fate as men.

Luke 11:46 King James Version

46 And he said, Woe unto you also, ye lawyers! for ye lade men with burdens grievous to be borne, and ye yourselves touch not the burdens with one of your fingers.

Luke 11:52 King James Version

52 Woe unto you, lawyers! for ye have taken away the key of knowledge: ye entered not in yourselves, and them that were entering in ye hindered.

Woe (wō/noun) is a noun for great sorrow or distress. Woe to you, lawyers. You burdened men with burdens that were too heavy to bear. You create bad rules and great sorrow for the unborn. Why do you do this lawyer's? You refrain from touching any of the burdens with your fingers. Does this imply that you are not ill impacted by the burdens? Because you and your progeny are not affected by the bad or severe rules that have been set up for the unborn. The laws you make are not applicable to your household as you are above the law. The key to knowledge has been taken away by you. And do not enter the key of knowledge into yourselves. Is this implying that the lawyer lacks knowledge of true law? Because it goes on to say, 'And those who were entering in you were hindered.' Hindered, past participle: To create difficulties for (someone or something), resulting in delay or obstruction. Is it plausible to suggest that your law practice is a hindrance to others due to your genuine interest in it, not just for the sake of it? Lawyers go on to become political figures, while others wait to become executors of the estates of high-profile entertainers. Everything is done for the sake of money. I need to keep my emotions under control. I was about to lose sight of the fact that I am writing about love.

"Something happened along the way. What used to be happy was sad. Something happened along the way. And yesterday was all we had. And oh, after the love has gone, how could you lead me on and not let me stay around."

Lyrics from the Earth Wind and Fire song "After The Love Has Gone."

As love sizzle for a bit, we're flying high. Sizzle is a term used to describe someone who is highly exciting or passionate, particularly when it comes to sexuality. What happens to the sizzle after the excitement, passion, and sexual arousal have faded? Our love stayed afloat because of the sizzle. Due to the dissipation of the sizzle. We are on the lookout for someone new to entice us. The title After Love is Gone refers to a loss of spark between the two individuals who were deeply infatuated with one another. After the love has disintegrated. After the excitement subsides. After the passion has faded. After sexual arousal has subsided. We begin to search for these things outside of our current relationship or marriage, hoping to satisfy a need or desire.

Love (love/lav/noun) an intense feeling of deep affection. "babies fill parents with feelings of love."

Similar: deep affection, fondness, tenderness, warmth, intimacy, attachment, endearment, devotion, adoration, passion, desire, worship, lust, yearning, infatuation, adulation, besottedness, compassion, care, caring, regard, solicitude, concern, friendliness, friendship, kindness, charity, goodwill, sympathy, kindliness, altruism, philanthropy, unselfishness, benevolence, brotherliness, sisterliness, fellow feeling, humanity, relationship, love affair, affair, romance, liaison, affair of the heart, intrigue, amour Opposite: hatred a great interest and pleasure in something.

Excitement (ex·cite·ment/ik ˈsītmant,ek asˈsītmant/noun) a feeling of great enthusiasm and eagerness."her cheeks were flushed with excitement.

Similar: exhilaration, elation, animation, enthusiasm, eagerness, anticipation, emotion, fire, fieriness, intensity, zeal, zest, pep, vim, zing, spark (Opposite: boredom, indifference) Something that arouses enthusiasm and eagerness; an exciting incident (plural noun: excitements)"the excitements of the previous night"

Similar: thrill, thrilling sensation, exciting sensation, adventure, treat, pleasure, delight, joy, kick, buzz, high, charge, sexual arousal.

What is sexual arousal? "Arousal is the feeling of being turned on sexually. When you're turned on, your body experiences physical and emotional changes."

Passion (pas·sion/'paSH(a)n/noun) strong and barely controllable emotion, relating to the instincts, physiological processes, and activities connected with physical attraction or intimate physical contact between individuals.

Examine how love, excitement, passion, and sexuality relate to each other. Considering how all of this can have an impact on the idea and concept of love. If we encounter this in our relationship. The moment it disappears. Our thoughts begin to question if he/she loves me in a genuine way. I feel that something is not right. There are indications of change in the behavior patterns. Your expressions of love, excitement, passion, and sexual arousal are all positive. All of a sudden, those actions come to a halt. When no one is willing to discuss it, the emotional roller coaster happens. The fact that two individuals no longer have a strong desire for one another is staggering. Their fear or conditioning to endure a situation that causes them to be reluctant to let each other go. Accepting a bad situation or living conditions out of fear is an ignorance of self-love. Self-love is defined by loving yourself before loving anyone else or anybody at all. Self-love is characterized by loving yourself first and foremost before loving anyone else. Brother, you know you made a mistake. Above all things, it is important to love God with all your being. This is true! But how can you love God in the same way as you love yourself? The act of loving oneself is equivalent to loving God. And to love God is to love oneself. Separating God from ourselves or ourselves from God is not a good thing. If God is to be loved. Through our existence, we should study, understand, and exercise the love of God.

In my opinion, the study of love should be conducted from a Scientific and mathematical point of view. Eliminating emotions from the core of analytical thinking analysis. Obtaining a final answer through intelligence from a scientific and mathematical perspective. To breathe new life into a world of solutions that we live in every day through our actions. It is our responsibility to avoid living in the prison of love. Discovering and comprehending that love is founded on freedom, justice, and equality. Acquire the book The Science of Love by John Baines. The first part of the book begins with the situations and examples of Corrupt Love. Part 2 addresses the question of 'What is love?' By reading this book, I was able to transcend my love emotions and discover the intelligence of love. Allowing scientific and mathematical intelligence to guide me when it comes to love. This provided me with a shield to protect myself in case of a battle. According to Pat Benatar, "love is a battlefield.

In my conclusion, should we operate according to the law of love? Should we operate based on the love concept that was learned in our childhood? Love is the essence of life, and living it requires love. Whose criteria should we follow to live our lives today? I am not implying that I infringe on the beliefs, faith, or way of life of other individuals. Our intelligence is sufficient to prevent obstacles from preventing us from exhibiting sound integrity and high moral character in treating another human being, person, place, or thing with the greatest respect and benevolence. Not allowing color, sex, gender, age, religion, money, and status to be the criteria for how we treat each other today. Not allowing a very low and degrading behavior to set precedent for high moral character. If you are in a high-ranking position and consider others less important because of their position or financial status. Your light has become dim, and it's about to go out completely. Enhance your light to improve the light of others. This method ensures that your light will never go out. Pass on the torch to the next person who is ablaze. The fire is a source of motivation that drives the spirit to achieve extraordinary things. We can make that extraordinary event a manifestation of self-respect and love for the entire world. Our children in this society watch us, learn, and live out what they see, as adults in this society. If we detect rebellion in them, are we the ones who made them rebel in the first place? With all the love that is present in the world. Is it possible for us to fine-tune our vision so that we can see equality and actually be and practice one love?

About The Author

Jasiyah Sherrieff Bey is a student of Noble Drew Ali's teachings. The Honorable Elijah Muhammad as taught by the Honorable Minister Louis Farrakhan. A student of the Hermetic Science Philosophy. His passion is reading philosophical works and the true history of Asiatic black men and women in America and throughout history.

In his own words, 'I will seek truth until my last breath.' I intend to work towards becoming a student of knowledge, wisdom, and understanding. The objective is to achieve a life of peace and contentment. At the same time, being prepared for conflict. Jasiyah has earned a bachelor's degree in digital filmmaking from The Los Angeles Film School, as well as an Associate's degree in exercise science. Throughout his childhood, he has had a strong imagination and a desire to use his mind. Alongside the many gifts and talents he has earned, he has also been a singer, songwriter, producer, and owner of businesses over the years. Jasiyah is continuing to develop the many gifts and talents that already exist in his being. He loves the life of peace and unity among people in all walks of life; he feels with the voice of reason. We are capable of sitting down with each other and reaching a mutual understanding to resolve conflicts. We must first make changes in ourselves in order to have the power to change the world.

www.ingramcontent.com/pod-product-compliance
Lightning Source LLC
Chambersburg PA
CBHW040845010826
48978CB00012BB/908